This book belongs to

D1314160

For my crazy family, whose storytelling
and adventures over the years have
provided much inspiration for this book!

ISBN 978-1-84135-996-0

Copyright © Laura Wall

All rights reserved. No part of this publication may be reproduced
or utilized in any form or by any means electronic or mechanical,
including photocopying, recording, or by any information storage
and retrieval system now known or hereafter invented, without
the prior written permission of the copyright holder.

First published 2013

Published by Award Publications Limited,
The Old Riding School, The Welbeck Estate,
Worksop, Nottinghamshire, S80 3LR

www.awardpublications.co.uk

13 1

Printed in China

Also available:

Goose
Goose Goes to School
Goose Goes to the Zoo
Happy Birthday, Goose!
Goose on the Farm

Goose Goes Shopping

by Laura Wall

AWARD PUBLICATIONS LIMITED

An envelope arrives for Sophie and Goose.

It's an invitation to Ben and Sam's party.

But Sophie has no party clothes to wear.

Or presents to give.

"We'll have to go to the shops," says Mum.

Goose has never been to the shops.

The shopping centre is very busy.

Goose spots a strange moving staircase.

And he puts a flappy foot on it.

Whooosh! Goose is whisked upwards.

As Sophie follows Goose up one side ...

... he comes down the other!

When Sophie catches up with Goose,

they spot something that looks like fun.

Wheeeeeeeee!

Mum, Sophie and Goose go into a bookshop.

Sophie and Goose find a great gift for Ben.

"Now let's have some lunch," says Mum.

Sophie orders a knickerbocker glory.

She shares it with Goose.
They both think it is very yummy indeed.

After lunch, they visit the toy shop.

Sophie finds a lovely pink doll's house.

And Goose makes some friends.

Sophie and Goose take their new friends

on a train ride round the toy shop.

And they all enjoy watching the pretty toy ferris wheel go round and round.

Then Goose finds a brilliant gift for Sam.

Now it's time to buy Sophie a party outfit.

First, Sophie needs some new shoes.

They find some nice hats, too.

"Oh, Goose! What a lovely hat!"

Then they make silly faces in a big mirror.

But Sophie still needs to find a new dress.

Mum and Sophie pick out a few to try on.

Sophie tries on a pink dress.

And then a blue one.

But none of them seem quite right. Until...

Perfect!

"It's time to go home," says Mum.

Goose helps Sophie to wrap
the gifts for Ben and Sam.

Excitedly they walk to the party with Mum.

"We hope you like your presents! We had lots of fun choosing them, didn't we, Goose?"

"Honk!" says Goose.